# nothing short of 100

selected tales from
100 Word Story

Outpost19 | San Francisco
outpost19.com


Published 2018 by Outpost19.


Faulkner, Grant; Mundell, Lynn; and Olsen, Beret, editors;
Nothing Short Of: Selected Tales from 100WordStory.org/ Grant Faulkner, Lynn Mundell, and Beret Olsen, editors
ISBN: 9781944853488 (pbk)

*OUTPOST19*

ORIGINAL
PROVOCATIVE
READING

# nothing short of 100

selected tales from
100 Word Story

# CONTENTS

# INTRODUCTION

*by Grant Faulkner, Lynn Mundell, and Beret Olsen*

What can a hundred words do? Deliver major drama? Plumb a juicy backstory? Linger on beautiful sensory minutiae? With many, many more words, novelists fill the capacious spaces of their pages with layers of details and a sense of expansion, putting bulk on their story's bones and strapping together their crisscrossing plot lines.

But what if a hundred words is all you've got—to do everything? To reveal a character's essence. To deliver telling moments. To take a reader's breath away. What if everything relied on hints, tiny details, and what's left out?

What different types of stories would arise if told through concision and compression—as if seeing through the fixed lens of a camera? Could an arbitrary word-count inspire compositional creativity?

These were the questions we asked ourselves in 2011 as we began this tiny venture, *100 Word Story*, which has ended up becoming a big thing. We were introduced to the 100-word form (often referred to as a "drabble") through Paul Strohm's collection of 100-word stories, *Sportin' Jack*, and we soon became addicted to writing 100-word stories ourselves. In this age of online distractions and fragmented attention spans, we thought a 100-word story was the perfect length to capture life, the perfect length to read. Our selections have been chosen for both the annual Best Small Fictions series and Wigleaf "best of" awards for short shorts. We decided to publish this collection of the very best stories in our first six years to show the many inventive ways writers have told stories within such a tiny compartment.

To write with such brevity seems like it should be easy, but it's not. Every word, every sentence matters. These miniature stories communicate via caesuras and crevices. There is no asking more, no premise of comprehensiveness, because the 100-word story is a form that favors excision over agglomeration. Nonetheless, the writers in this anthology will take you to highways, beaches, bars, and freak shows, into bedrooms, and to faraway lands. You'll meet lovers—young and old—children, animals, tormentors, memories, an inflatable girlfriend, and ghosts—characters conjured into three-dimensions from a single gesture, a turn of phrase, the sparest of details.

Writer Deb Olin Unferth says, "The short makes

us consider such questions as: What is the essential element of 'story'? How much can the author leave out and still create a moving, complete narrative? If I remove all back story, all exposition, all proper nouns, all dialogue—or if I write a story that consists only of dialogue—in what way is it still a story?"

Over the years, it's amazed us to read wildly differing answers to these questions, all fitting within a 100-word box. The restriction to 100 words is similar to the requirements of a poetic form—whether it's a sonnet, a villanelle, or a haiku. Such constraints make the creative act more difficult, yet push the writer to look beyond obvious associations and consider different words that fit into the rhyming or iambic scheme. Likewise with the requirement to use precisely 100 words. Imaginative leaps don't necessarily happen by thinking "outside the box" as the popular saying goes, but within the box. In this collection, you'll find "Snapshots of a Crash," in which writer Melanie Taylor Herrera follows a clock backward to tell what set in motion a tragedy. With "The White Album," by Lee Romer Kaplan, young lovers are introduced, separated, and reunited in middle age. Ashley Chantler gives us a glimpse into stream-of-consciousness to hilarious effect in "A Day in the Life of Steve."

The stories in this collection call attention to the

spectral blank spaces left around stray moments. The gaps within and around the stories—the gaps between words, sentences, and paragraphs, the gaps around a story itself—speak as large as the texts themselves. "Is not the most erotic portion of the body where the garment gapes?" wrote Roland Barthes in *Pleasure of the Text.* It's in those gapes where the vaporous whorls of suspense reside.

Shorts require immediacy; they're a flicker of light in the darkness, a pinprick, a thunderclap. The writer has to hone focus, to practice a Zen-like concentration in a way that longer pieces don't require because they privilege the layering of detail and exposition. Telling a good flash story is similar to playing the Ouija board. You discover a small part of the story and let your imagination communicate with the other side to know the rest of it.

Concision is the quiet stepchild of the writing family. It's Cinderella. It doesn't cry out for attention, and its benefits are easily forgotten because writers generally prove their worth with more words. But what is hinted at or even left out can be as key in making a story work as any promulgation of words. The most haunting stories are those that don't provide answers, but open up questions. As Ku Ling wrote, "A good short-short is short but not small, light but not slight."

# ELLA: THEN

*by Tara Lynn Masih*

Ella likes things tiny. Tiny toy dishes, tiny dolls. She even wants her dad to be tiny. Like the Incredible Shrinking Man she saw on the Telly. He could live in her Lincoln Log Cabin.

Ella has a tiny pet. From her dad's Ronson cigarette lighter, a flint. Red. Blowing the bead across the floor, she takes it for a walk. Till it falls in a canyon between floorboards. He won't give her another.

Ella's father does not shrink to a point of control. He smokes, stares, strokes, rolls her around. She goes tiny and red to disappear in cracks.

# HARD TIME

*by Courtney Watson*

Joe ordered his first kit from a hobby magazine sent to his cell mate. The house was an antebellum plantation with a blue-papered bathroom and white columns. It had staircases and a library full of tiny books with real pages. The house was populated by little doll people, also ordered from the back pages, who would never, ever in their little doll lives rob the doll bank, armed with a tiny doll gun, shoot two of the doll tellers, and be sent to doll prison. It just wouldn't happen. Not when they had a place like this to call home.

# CHICKEN DANCE

*by Misty Ellingburg*

I went to the exhibit; I met everyone in U of I's indigenous drum group and asked their names and Tribal affiliation, stating mine. A handsome singer, a Coeur d'Alene Chicken Dancer, drove me home and told me bad rez jokes, *Blasphemy* by Sherman Alexie on the floor of his beat-up pick-up. My, my.

He told me, "You're beautiful; come be beautiful around me."

Later, he fucked me, his intensive thrusting in no way indicative of his dance training, his sweet singing, and I was sorry for it, and dry as the prairies where he danced with all that passion.

# THE CEMENT HEART

*by Cornelia Nixon*

He had been gone four years, when I looked down in my own driveway and saw in the cement a heart with an arrow crudely drawn, his initials at the top, a plus sign, and then mine. When did he do that, and why didn't I see it until now? I find his writing on my recipes. On the one for zucchini quiche, he added: Smother in pork chops, bake two hours. If I wrote Use Fresh next to something canned, he wrote Use Hundred Year Old by the next ingredient. Messages in a bottle from a vanished planet now.

# BOB AND BETTY

*by Molly Giles*

It was a good divorce. They each took one of the cars and one of the labradoodles; they divided the silver, antiques, and paintings, put the house up for sale, agreed to split the proceeds, and were shaking hands goodbye when they heard a musical tinkle from the garden. "Oh-oh," she remembered, "my wind chimes." "My wind chimes," he corrected. They hurried across the lawn and reached for the chimes at the exact same moment; when she tripped him, he slugged her, when he slugged her, she bit him. The realtor found their bodies later, chimes twined around their throats.

# RECEPTIVE

*by Kona Morris*

He said he liked to be scientific about it. Stick his finger in and feel around. "What's that?" "This part is really soft." "I feel ripples."

He called her "receptive." She wanted it to mean he thought she was a great lover, but it didn't feel like that's what it meant.

Would he call her "receptive" if she lay still, stiff legged and unbending? It bothered her how unaware he was of her role, less valued than the anemone she followed over jagged rocks to see. He poked its center and reeled with excitement at how fast it closed.

# KYOTO

*by Jacques Debrot*

In Kyoto you attend a lavish, decadent dinner for which you've paid a small fortune to eat off the body of a beautiful woman. Like the others at your table, you clap when she's wheeled in and make hazy murmurs of appreciation until the old scarecrow on your left abruptly lifts a piece of tuna from her throat. Next, a nipple is revealed. A red toenail. Now it's your turn. For a moment you deliberate, then remove a rose petal from her stomach. The skin you've exposed is damp and white. The navel, a small crater on a soft moon.

# FULL-LENGTH MIRROR

*by Paul Strohm*

Claire has been wanting a full-length mirror in our New York apartment. How come, I want to know. You can look at your top half in the bathroom and you see your feet any time in the shoestore. But it's the overview she wants, the ensemble. So we head for Gracious Home and carry one back on the subway. I start wondering whether there might be something for me in this deal after all. Suppose, I say, we put it here, next to the bed? She doesn't think so. Why not? Next to the bed, she says, might be counterproductive.

# A CATHOLIC CHURCH

*by Royce Jeffrey*

The sign outside proclaimed:

-CHURCH PARKING ONLY-

*God Forgives.*

*Kowalski and Sons Towing does not.*

Father Timothy would've smiled.

He once warned that hell had a room with my name on it after I accidentally scratched his gold Cadillac while carrying the plastic baby Jesus statue to the nativity scene.

I asked if my room would be close to his. He loathed me, and I avoided him like meat on Fridays. Poor Timothy. He died at an after-mass mixer; keeled over mid-sentence into the sugar cookies and lemonade.

His nephew got the Cadillac. Stuck on a colorful, "Pro-Choice" bumper sticker.

# THREE RNs ON THEIR LUNCH BREAK

*by J. Eldon Hauck*

In the photograph engraved on his tombstone he looked so young, stumping us, because, while he was younger than us, he'd always struck us as an old soul. Jen touched where the rough engraving of his hair gave way to the smooth black granite. What wasn't in the photograph was us in the booth around him, happy hour, numbing ourselves with cosmo-ritas, having lost one. We recalled how badly we'd wanted laughter and how, when the alcohol landed, it came. We'd been cropped out, red eyes, scrubs and all. Although we knew we weren't supposed to take offense, we did.

# SNAPSHOTS OF A CRASH

*by Melanie Taylor Herrera*

11:00 I close my eyes. 10:55 Lights are coming right at us. 10:50 I put my hand on Kareem's face, he bites my palm fiercely, and loses his grip of the wheel. 10:30 His accusations and my explanations become an entangled sound mass, screaming and crying. 10:00 Kareem's silence engulfs us both. 9:55 The car speeds through heavy traffic. 9:50 Kareem almost runs over an elderly couple. I turn my head and keep looking at them until they disappear into the distance. 9:30 My voice sounds alien, like I'm talking under water, while I confess: "Yes, I slept with Carlos."

# APOLOGIA IN ABSENTIA

*by JC Reilly*

It was not my intention to purloin your glass eye: I saw it on the nightstand as you dozed, my little cyclops. Iris green as the North Atlantic, pupil black as cuttlefish ink. Something to remember you by, I think, pocketing it and scuttling home, where its potential for décor is assured. How it will gleam on the neon wicker buffet, next to the first-edition *Dianetics*, a bust of Jackie Chan, an Ewok teapot, the jackalope I skinned myself. An eye for an I.... Surely that macaroni necklace I presented you on our third date will prove a fair exchange?

# SIDESHOW

*by Thaisa Frank*

The sideshow's latest attraction is Brad, a darkly handsome electrician, and his chocolate poodle Rex. They sleep in a featherbed and snore in perfect rhythm. Last summer Brad's wife kicked him out because of his snoring and Brad's grief was so immense it inspired Rex to synchronize his snores. It was only a matter of time before a talent scout heard them through an open window and the show was packed. Sometimes Brad's ex-wife sneaks in. She trembles with the brilliant thunder of each snore, ignores the rapt, adoring women. *I heard this first*, she whispers to the popcorn-scented dark.

# WEDDING PARTY MOVED TO THE CEMETERY AT MIDNIGHT

*by Joshua Michael Stewart*

*For Bret & Sydney*

The bride floats between the stones. Her groom plays dead for an iPhone camera. Laughter spills from mouths sweet with spirits. A plaid blazer dances with a pearl necklace. The groom plants a fat kiss on his new wife's lips under a marble angel with a chipped wing. The trills of spring peepers serenade the souls and all of the plastic flowers. And the departed do not weep, harping on their marriages to stillness. Instead they sing, Ob-La-Di, Ob-La-Da, in their NYC-apartment-sized plots, happy to be invited. It's been so long since any of them have been to a party.

# DRIVE FAST, TAKE CHANCES

*by Tom Hazuka*

Fitz threw a good party. I only left because I never linger till the downside of anything. I was nearly to my car when Fitz yelled, "Drive fast, take chances!"

I turned and saw him grinning on the porch, arm around my ex-girlfriend Karen. Despite the potential for awkwardness there was none. We're amicable adults with suitable loose grips on history.

They waved goodbye and I waved back, pondering a response—"Words to live by!"—but decided to swallow it. Karen rested her head on Fitz's shoulder, but not until I drove away. I only saw it in my rearview.

# COFFEE BEAN

*by Oren Peleg*

Pretty Asian girl asks if she can sit across from me. Yes. Her bangs almost cover her eyes. She steals glances. I've never stolen anything. Not even a candy bar. Condoms from the health center don't count. I steal glances back. I lower my laptop screen. It's been almost a year since I've gotten lai—Not important. *Can I buy you a coffee?* That'll work. Here we go. Moment of tru—moment of boyfriend entrance. He bends down like a sauropod eating a plant. He kisses her sloppily right there across from me. I lied. It's been almost two years.

# FATE ON THE HIGHWAY

*by Karen Benke*

Driving back from the beach, I talk to my dead father. Tell him what happened before doesn't have to happen again. We reminisce over his schemes. As usual, I'm doing all the talking—that hotdog stand he built, the solar panels on the roof, his days with measuring tape in hand. The familiar silence merges between us same as always. Adrift in the night, I accelerate past all doubt that he no longer loves me. I follow a trail of taillights out across the bridge and there he is: thumb in the air, hitching a ride through my mind.

# ON THE TYE

*by Maud Casey*

Inside his disastrous apartment, exuberant files: Mousetraps; Buttons; Inkwells; Santa Claus Outfits; Fountains for Your Faucet. Old letters—"frankness in a man is an unusual thing but frankness in a woman as beautiful as you…" A bill for 26 years of unpaid dues from a New York gentlemen's club. Fifteen years after the Parkinson's diagnosis—by then, crawling up and down stairs—he and my mother went tubing on the Tye River. He would remember it the rest of his life, he said 10 days before he died. His body anchored and buoyant, the sunlit water returning it to him.

# HIGHWAY KIND

*by Kate Hill Cantrill*

I called him Ant-nee. He wore a snake of plastic vein within his arm to save his kidney. He and I, we sculpted plants. He had a way with succulents; did the driving to the homes needing beauty. On the way he'd stop for men along the medium, give them dollars, search their eyes. I asked him why for every one. I joked and said his karma was clear by now. He turned the radio up, gunned the engine, said, Who knows which one might be my Pop? One day, he said. One day I'll see mine eyes in his.

# ADULT THEATER

*by Tupelo Hassman*

I bought my best friend a singing telegram, a Peewee Herman impersonator. It turned out he was a transvestite meth head living in one room, hung wall to wall with dresses. I know this because at the last minute he called, asking for a ride to the gig. He'd gotten into a fistfight with his lover who took the car. It's open, he said softly, still curled on the couch, the eye of a storm of tulle. In the car, I pretended not to notice him covering a shiner as he reapplied his rouge, that the birthday balloons said, It's a Girl!

# DARKNESS, OKLAHOMA CITY, 1996

*by Brian Castleberry*

To have something to do, they drove around the city after nightfall listening to music. Beastie Boys. Digable Planets. Some fuzzy mixed tape a DJ sold before leaving for St. Louis. They would end up at Denny's smoking cigarettes and drinking coffee, talking William S. Burroughs and waiting for the guy to show with a sack. A waitress there wanted to be a model and Dylan screwed her in the back of a car in the parking lot one Tuesday dawn. She got stoned with him in the front seat after. She moved away, too. All the way to Seattle.

# CONFESSIONS OF A FORMER SKINHEAD

*by Becky Tuch*

We were only boys. Spike-hearted teenagers with round rescue-me eyes. We threaded our Docs with fat red laces. Our hair fell in piles, skulls shiny as eggs. We rolled in tattooed crews. We spread white wings the size of infinity, sprayed names on subway cars. We threw bottles, hid rolls of quarters in our fists, wiped blood from our eyes. Our mothers didn't recognize us. We were fists clenched tight, black wheels spinning. We were music, hard and loud and lit up from inside. It was 1987. We were only boys, and it was all we knew how to be.

# STREETS AT NIGHT

*by Lee L. Krecklow*

We took to the streets and to the rooftops high on inhalants and high on each other and high on ourselves, high with the confidence of a victory over everything we had yet to become and could not imagine becoming but which we always knew could befall us when light came, if not that morning then perhaps the next or even five thousand daybreaks away, but no mistake could be made about the threat of dawn, so in the darkest hours before it reached its pale fingers over the horizon and clawed at our swollen eyes, we made everything ours.

# WEED

*by Jane Ciabattari*

She was good at trimming. Fastidious.

He paid her $879 in cash. On time.

But he was getting weird.

He wanted her truck.

He went into Yreka for coffee every morning. Forty minutes away on the winding road. He was a creature of habit, even when all cranked up.

He chopped up a couple of OxyContin pills on the kitchen counter before leaving. He dropped the keys to her truck. She slid them into her bra, a quick flick as if adjusting a strap, and she held them safe next to her heart.

If he backed up his car, she was free.

# ON THE ART OF JILTING

*by Ruth Martini*

You are unfaithful to the principles of *Breathless* by Godard he says to you. He is teaching you the Art of Jilting, Introduction to Hipster Courtship. He means this remark to be cutting. You understand that until you have repented of your uncouthness and been baptized in the French New Wave you cannot be saved. You went to see *Breathless* with this boy who found Jane Austen trite. You should've said then that her parlor miniatures captured a macrocosm of human interactions in the cross-hairs of her cross-stitches. You should have stalked off with your parasol clipped under your arm.

# SECONDHAND

*by MJ Iuppa*

What I heard over the thrum of washing machines and dryers was complaint. She says to no one, he loved anchovies more than her, then rolls her eyes and sets loose a whistle that wheezes into a cough. She's too thin to be pregnant, carrying her basket of faded underwear, next to her swollen belly, the shape of a goldfish bowl. She wants to leave this one trailer park town and go to Florida. She folds her underwear into tiny triangles. She finds a pair of orange pants left in a dryer. Perfect, she says, something new to wear out.

# MARTHA

*by Chad Hanson*

Sophie left Chicago for Panama City, Florida. She made the trip every year, toward the end of February. In Panama, she ate burgers. She watched game shows. She went to flea markets. This time she found a leather belt. Amid imprints of bison tooled onto the belt, somebody stamped the letters: M-A-R-T-H-A. She wore the belt to the lounge at the inn. A suitor saw her by the bar. He said, "Martha?" She did not correct him. She let him take Martha out to a honky-tonk. Sophie didn't know how to dance to that type of music, but Martha knew.

# WHERE THE STARS FALL TOGETHER

*by James Braziel*

They make a pool of silver, swim as stones through the pine branches, push back needles like a dog's fur shaking off the bathwater and carry what is left of the sky as bones hitched together into a stream. It never tires. The stars so still are never really still. And what pieces you can hold—thread, whiskey, chigger bites, sin—you lose like the loosest water round and round your fingers, like her hair you cannot touch now, like the last bits of light you mapped on the bed until worn blind-through, sleepless, breath-rattled, loping through the dark alone.

# BREATH

*by Eric Prochaska*

The first warm breath mitigates her melancholy. I sustained my young love through another winter. She's at the park. Canopy of still barren branches. Learning how her legs have atrophied, struggling to expand lungs against sharp jabs. She won't run more than a mile. But she won't be home for hours. Shirtless grad students playing Frisbee. She'll stop, stretch by a nearby picnic table. Smooth white chests. Sit, lean back, rest her elbows atop the table. Her thankful grin sunward, eyes closed. Perked nipples. Her chest stretching the years-old t-shirt. She won't come home for hours. Coffee on her breath.

# A CHANGE OF CLOTHES

*by Robert Scotellaro*

Widows are beautiful, he thought. So covered in need they shimmered. This was his third. She lay under a sheet, which had a hole burnt into it earlier from a pot seed exploded from a joint. The size of a lizard's eye. His suits suit you, she said. A little tight in the shoulders, but not so bad. Her cat rubbed against him, as if nothing had changed. He turned this way and that in the long mirror. Reached for a silk suit on a hanger. She rolled another, using a credit card to separate the seeds out this time.

# THICKER THAN WATER

*by Jean-Luc Bouchard*

I took my grandfather out to dinner for his birthday, because it seemed the proper thing to do. Neither of us particularly wanted to go to dinner together, but since he was alone and I happened to be visiting town during his birthday, I felt compelled to insist. My grandfather and I don't have much in common; he's a retired arms dealer, I am a circus clown. But after some torturous small talk concerning weather and health, as the meal began, we were finally able to come together as family in the way we treated our waitress like total shit.

# MY INFLATABLE GIRLFRIEND

*by Dan Campbell*

Today she's a hot cheerleader, the next day she's dressed like a nun. She knows me, she's a mind reader. Yes, plastic dolls are lots of fun. I'm hoping she lasts till December, that's when the warranty expires. If not I'll date her twin sister who's stored beside the snow tires. She's happy with cheap perfume and she doesn't talk all day. I've met the perfect woman, there's nothing more I can say. My castles and girlfriends are inflatable and my backyard swimming pool is, too. Friends say my tastes are debatable and I tell them to kiss my taboo.

# IN BLACKEST NIGHT

*by Kevin Sharp*

Midnight. Comics & Comix. Pop color superheroes in the dark. You ditched the party, brought her into this sacred space with your sacred employee key. She kept saying *awesome*. Now, huddled close on the floor, whispering like it's a library or a funeral home. Over her shoulder, the G's: Green Arrow, Green Lantern. Her with green eyes would be some kind of poetry; instead they're big and butterscotch and blinking up at you. If love is having nowhere you'd rather be, no one you'd rather be with, then this is it. Confess your heart? Kiss her? What would Batman do?

# PART-TIME DREAMER

*by Maggie Bohara*

After we fight, I dream I'm milking a cow and the udder tastes like mint chocolate. Dream-You says the milk tastes regular, sour even. I say it's a miracle.

Over pancake breakfast, I tell you that Mary Shelley, only nineteen, dreamed of Frankenstein. You say she died of a brain tumor at fifty-three.

Last night, I joined a circus. And my grandfather—the one who drank—was clown and lion tamer. In the tent, it snowed warm snow. And you were kneeling, drawing computer codes in the powder. From the tightrope, I read your language but couldn't understand your meaning.

# AT LARGE

*by Barrett Warner*

I pretend fate is a dog. Not a retriever. Nor is fate a working dog; fate has never worked a day in its life. And not a shepherd or a dobie. Fate doesn't bark at mailmen or catch Frisbees.

Fate is a simple dog, bored, just wanders in, and leaves without a stir. Sometimes fate grunts, but doesn't growl when I tenderly kick to see if it is awake.

And because it's a dog, it makes cocked faces when I ask it why, why?

So I put the bowl of water on the porch. In the morning it's always gone.

# WHAT DO *THOSE* CHARACTERS WANT?

*by Pamela Painter*

Well, I will tell you: They want to know why some characters get long stories while they get Micro, Sudden, Flash. Why some characters get cities or towns, streets, homes with dog houses and dogs that howl in the night. Why those homes have rooms that matter, dining rooms where plates are broken or someone opens an aged Bordeaux, bedrooms where lust gives way to murder or love. They want scenes awash in back story, then the rush of rapids, steep falls, or floods. They want it to lead to something that is something else. But not in a Flash.

# DIVORCE PARTY

*by Marc J. Sheehan*

Friends gave us towels with "Not His" and "Not Hers" written in glittery epoxy, mismatched wine glasses, and CDs in the wrong jewel cases. Eric, a mail-order minister, oversaw our anti-vows and we exchanged plastic gumball machine rings. A year later my ex took a job out of state—a move I blessed out of stupidity and a misunderstanding of the Buddhist tenet of nonattachment. Sometimes, when the hamper is full and the Laundromat too awful to contemplate, I use the "Not Hers" towel, whose words are so rough they leave long, unromantic scratches if I forget to avoid them.

# A LESSON PLAN

*by Kayleb Rae Candrilli*

The woman taught her daughters at home. Homeschooled. Homeschoolers. She taught them how to sentence diagram and to read the map of the world—plastered big against the wall, eight feet wide and six feet tall. She taught them how to dance dirty, a secret to hide from her husband. She held the lesson locked in the laundry room, on rough poured concrete. Dirty dancing and dirty laundry airing. The woman played for her daughters Will Smith's "Miami" and rolled her hips. When the word sexy came, her daughters gasped. She said, sexy isn't a bad word, just an adjective.

# WHAT ARE YOU SELLING?

*by Lisa Rubenson*

The shoe store man who wears shiny brown suits and looks like Scott Baio came to my leg warmer kiosk yesterday with an Orange Julius. I figure he'll ask me out tonight, so I cut class to lay out. "Bain de Soleil for the St. Tropez tan": the gel smells sweet and dangerous, blood mixed with oranges. It reminds me of the sex I haven't had yet, of skinny girls and European men. Of all the things I will resent when I am older. I spread it on my shoulders, but it's too late—the flesh there is already burned.

# FINAL TALLY

*by Cathy Safiran*

We sat on the ledge at the overlook [Skyline Boulevard]; crushed cans of Special X and Budweiser, contemplated lengths of rope [right there; a flock of swans taking flight]. She told me she was a hand-me-down, she'd confess to anyone's sins; [a black V swings over the bridge heading north]; at midnight in the middle of summer she became the way the truth the light of my life [the V is a thin line, a speck]. You tell me longing is a tree, rooted and heaven-bound; say everything can be measured: sadness and silence; the distance between loss and redemption.

# SISTER'S BOYFRIEND

*by Meg Tuite*

Sister shoves a handful of Triscuits down my throat. Pinned down by her legs I thrash and gag. Mom is passed out on the couch, empty bottles of pink Chablis beneath her. The psycho animation of New York's torrential roar blasts out of the TV while a sequined ball drops into Time Square where the masses celebrate another year to forget.

You kissed him, sister screeches, as I gasp for air, wheat splinters foaming out.

She doesn't know I whispered no when he snuck in my room. She doesn't know I threw up after he buckled his pants and left.

# ROYALTY

*by Kevin Catalano*

Just out of high school and looking for her lot, Queenie Ladd went after Big Paul King, manager of the Bojangles in town. She married him, despite his blazing eczema and constant smell of fried chicken and hush puppies. She stayed with him, despite his pill-popping and fooling around with Inez, the lady who made the biscuits. And now, four years and twice as many biscuit employees later, she's still with him, because as she'd been reminding her mama ever since Queenie quit sleeping on King's couch, "I just know some good luck's coming my way for bringing our names together."

# ABANDONMENT

*by Tonya Shenandoah*

A daughter cuts her long hair with a butter knife and places her heart inside a turtle shell. Loaded on vodka she passes out in an alley behind a bar where Trickster plants his seed inside her. She births a daughter, wraps her in burdock leaves and paper beer bottle labels and leaves her at the Indian Health Services doorstep. The young mother washes her face in her tears and wipes them over her baby's cheeks. As she walks away, strawberries sprout and blossom around her daughter. At the edge of the reservation, the mother turns into a monarch butterfly.

# THE SILVER DANIO

*by Jeremy Hawkins*

Boy and Girl meet in the river, and when Girl points with seductive slowness at a school of silver danio, Boy dives in to capture one. He places the fish in her hand, and she brings it near her face, feels its muscles twist, smells its glimmering scent. Later, Boy grows into Man. Often he wonders if Girl remembers him. The answer: Yes. Girl has established a tradition of baking elaborate fish dishes every Tuesday for her family. And often, when her husband kisses her, she remembers Boy's particular lust and the twisting of the small fish in her hand.

# FIVE THINGS

*by Manuel Gonzales*

I want to tell her the five most important things she needs to know before she leaves, but we haven't spoken all morning.

I made the coffee without being asked. She took it the same way.

I say five, but there could be more.

I'm sure there are more, but five is a good, round number, I think. Enough but not too many, not too many things to carry with her. She wouldn't listen beyond five, anyway.

A calm has settled over her. I say five, but really, there's only one thing, only one thing to tell her. Don't go.

# USELESS THINGS

*by Ariel Berry*

Forgetting the uses for things was, in a way, a relief. It was less painful, for instance, when her grandmother's teacups shattered on the tile floor. They seemed to have fulfilled their purpose. She wiped up the mess, then tied the wet washrag in her hair. She was no longer afraid to drive backwards, or paint her clothes, or weed indiscriminately. It was now impossible to make a mistake. As she lifted the hot kettle and embraced it, tea splashed onto her bare legs. These burns are what I was made for, she thought. These marks are who I am.

# A GUIDE TO SURVIVING MONOTONY

*by Alyssa Jordan*

Carve out the stone of a peach, tap the clay pipe against the sink, wrap your hands in bandages and bleed. Smile and cut the fruit into sweet meat pieces. Try not to mind when more than one hand pulls at your skin. Ignore the phone; ignore his smile when he answers. Pretend his face isn't full of cracks and lines and his voice no longer sounds like summer winds smoked by ash and sunlight. Tell yourself it doesn't hurt that much. Wait just a few more days before you leave. Pretend you are capable of being more than this.

# WE KNOW SO LITTLE ABOUT ICELAND

*by Kyle Hemmings*

I sat next to a stranger at The Octopus Bar. She had long grey hair, a freakishly young face, a body as lithe as a yoga teacher. I noticed the fingertips of her right hand were blackened. She caught me staring. She confessed it was from the second to last lover. "He was too hot for me. The last one was too kind." She later spoke about her stepmother's country—Iceland. "What's the interior like? The northernmost edge? Can polar bears commit suicide? Why?" At a diner, I sat between two empty stools, ordered black coffee. It burnt my lips.

# MOVING SALE

*by Janice D. Soderling*

I was being mean all morning so she would stop nagging we should get married. She is being nice back. She spots two trophy heads with antlers, "Cute! Mr. and Mrs. Deer!" I laugh, "Are you stupid or what? Only bucks have horns." I smirk. An oversized cowboy leans out of the garage. "This dude harassing you?" His voice is honey. Suddenly I see her with his eyes, her hair piled high, pretty face, tears. I say, "Whoa!" She looks back at him the same way. She steps away from me. "Yes, he is." All I can say is "Whoa!"

# OPEN ROADS

*by Ilan Greenberg*

He ran knuckles along the Formica like a traveling music man practicing invisible scales. From behind the counter she slapped down an insurance form. You reserved a sub-compact but we have larger cars on the lot, she said. I usually rent a small one—I'm not going far, he replied. She kept looking, as this was no answer. So he asked, do you have a convertible, something flashy? But in truth he wanted any car so long as he could eat in it messily. Maybe stain the seat with ketchup from a drive-thru burger joint. Freedom isn't driving. It's renting.

# HUMPTY DUMPTY

*by Elizabeth Swann*

There he sits in boxers, black birds perched alongside. How to explain a husband, babbling and unbalanced, high on the garden wall? The Missus is hatching a plan to send Humpty packing. Bills litter the table; he can't keep a job—comes home drunk and boiling. The first time Humpty scaled the wall, she ran outside in her slip to talk him down. After his fall, cops scrambled through daisies to find pieces to patch Humpty up. Back then he'd had a full head of hair. Sure, he was fragile, but she'd never noticed that crack forking between his eyes.

# SEAMS

*by Dane Holweger*

A zaftig teen peddled her younger sister's bike awkwardly up Highland Avenue at sunset. The young woman's body fought the seams of her aqua leotard. Dime-size sequins splashed disco on everything she passed. The effect was that of the Sparkletts water truck in flip-flops. Her body was not hers. The way her clothes fit proved it every day now. Boys were not staring at her but at something that had happened to her like an accident. Reaching Melrose, winded, she turned around. Coasting back she suddenly felt like a blur. It was as close to disappearing as she could get.

# PRACTICING

*by Roxanne Barber*

My best friend Vicki and I spent hours dressing up in her mother's discarded evening wear, carefully choosing cocktail dresses, costume jewelry, and high heels from the trunk in the garage. We expertly adjusted outfits to our 7-year-old bodies, tucking chiffon under cinched belts so we wouldn't trip. The object of our efforts lived near the end of the cul-de-sac. We strutted down the sidewalk, hoping he would emerge and be dazzled, make his choice. Eight-year-old boys are blind to haute couture. Just as well. I would return later in my cutoffs and Keds and have him all to myself.

# ANGELIQUE

*by Ulrica Hume*

She is an old soul. We talk of Barbie dolls and school. Her hands weaving stories. Maybe a hesitant smile. Eyes soft, earth-brown pansies, sadly martyred.

An old man steers his car up a hill. Passes through hoops of sky before powerlessly plunging. On the news I hear about the other cars, the domino effect. Little girl trapped inside.

Her father waits that night for her to return. Pacing, as if she is on a first date. Bronze shows through the drapes, a ring of light like a burning candle. Benediction. Dreams like honey. He leaves the porch light on.

# NOTE TO A GHOST

*by Peg Alford Pursell*

After you died I wandered the nearby field. Twilight. Your cat ran up to me with a bird's heart in its mouth. I wanted to make something more out of that than what it was. You know what it was. The way you knew to let out your first cry: how you were there and not, how it's a witness who hears and translates your feelings expressed in the tone. It's only natural, as in leaves abandoning the trees to fall at your feet, as is the bleeding red moon this night, scientifically explicable. Beast, bird, botany, being, all knowable.

# GLYPH

*by Robert Shapard*

He'd loved hieroglyphs ever since Indiana Jones twisted one, a stone temple figure, and the walls rumbled open. Now he was just a guy with a sputtering Ducati motorcycle taking business classes who fell in love with a girl, and took a poetry class to be with her. He learned all glyphs, hiero or otherwise, were images, which could take form in any of the senses, so her scent in bed was a glyph, her touch was sometimes a glyph, and between her lips when she said goodbye, though he pleaded for her not to, his name was a glyph.

# THE CLOCK

*by Elizabeth Hazen*

The month she asks him to leave there are signs: earthquake, hurricane, a dead rabbit on the threshold. In retellings, she will claim to have buried the corpse, but in truth she scoops it with a shovel, puts it out with the next day's trash. For weeks she arranges and rearranges piles—plates, cutlery, bedding, photographs—as if solving a complex equation. The day of his departure, the mantel clock stops. Inside, the dead cell oozes into gears, and though she scrapes away the corrosion, a new battery is not enough. Still, the hours pass, though not exactly as before.

# THE HIVE

*by Ingrid Jendrzejewski*

We're buzzing in our pews, the electricity of raw gossip flitting around us like so many wings. We feed on it, spread it around like a honey that sticks. Our madam archdeacon is at the center of it all, and if the rumors are true, no vestment can hide her guilt from the likes of us.

The service is about to start. The organ hums to life, signaling the start of the processional: the venerable queen is about to emerge. Suspicion thickens the air like pollen. Our faces turn towards the narthex, primed to sting. Conditions are favorable for swarming.

# CAVING

*by Kendra Fortmeyer*

We have been in the cave for many months, long enough for Olive to fall in love with Lynette, and for Yolanda to miscarry, and Brynn to grow an extra set of teeth. It is the first that frightens us most. In the dark you can have a baby or not a baby, and darkness always contains too many teeth. But we were not prepared for the melding of bodies in the black: how you stop understanding where the yielding flesh of you begins and where, in the blindness, the bright spark of another flares up like a wild poppy.

# OLD MEN

*by Jeff Friedman*

In the middle of the afternoon, old men lose their gravity, floating off sidewalks. Some bump their heads against tree trunks. Some collide with birds, who resent intruders in their air space. Some old men get their filaments of hair tangled in branches while others wisely latch onto clouds and kick their way through the atmosphere. Some old men turn over and over in space, their wallets and keys dropping from their pockets. And others shoot up like hot air balloons. But on the ground, two old men clutch fire hydrants as if they were lovers and won't let go.

# GREAT COMPOSERS OF THE AMERICAN POPULAR SONG

*by Lina Chern*

A window opens on a forest: trees, moonlight, a path. You've been here before: the knot in a pine becomes a long-lost face, the veil of leaves a scarf of blue silk. You startle a flock of birds into flight and their cries echo a song playing in a tiny room wreathed in cigarette smoke. Through the window, the man at the piano sees a large house in a small town, his grandmother's tulips, the fall of his sister's hair. At the word song his eyes meet yours and his fingers pause on the keys: birds over a starlit canyon.

# THE STATE OF THINGS

*by Joe Dornich*

When the conversation turns from her mother's health—new medications, new side effects, same ailments—to Carol's love life, there is a pause. She audibly sighs into the receiver, pinches the meat between her eyes. Even though it will break her mother worse than the osteoporosis that is crippling her bones, Carol will try to explain the state of things. Somehow, it has reached the point where the most enjoyable aspect about going to a bar and meeting a guy and going home with him is that when she finally gets back to her apartment, her bed is already made.

# SWEETIE PIE

*by Sherrie Flick*

I started calling both my dog and husband Sweetie Pie the same year my husband found my lover's cashmere sock. I had stuffed it in my coat pocket after tugging at it nestled like a snake down my pants leg. But it escaped flaccidly onto our stone entryway. After my dog walk up and around the hill, the city nestled below us, its rivers aquiver, I unhooked the leash. I said, "Oh, Sweetie Pie. I'll always love you." Then, as the dog skittered to his kibble, I saw my husband's hand and the fine knit. I said, "Oh, Sweetie Pie."

# COMPETITION

*by Meg Pokrass*

She let him make love to her the first night and he told her that he would do this every single night for the rest of her life. She let him make love to her the next night, but it had already become some kind of contest in his mind about whether or not he could do this exactly as well as the night before. She let him make love to her the third night, but she was no longer there inside her body. Instead, she was watching from a safe distance—sitting next to the dog, catching her breath.

# CASSIOPEIA

*by Jacqueline Doyle*

He made his move in the planetarium. She'd been gazing up at the outlines of Cassiopeia in the night sky, squinting to see a queen on a throne. She looked down and saw him on his knees, squeezed in front of the folding seat beside her. Did you lose something? she said. Will you marry me? he asked, holding out the ring. She laughed. She couldn't help herself. What would she tell their children? Your father has always been ridiculous? Or maybe he'd tell the story. Your mother was always an arrogant bitch. Either way, she had to say no.

# INVITE HIM IN, ASK FOR HELP

*by Simon Jimenez*

The zipper began at the nape of her neck. With thumb and forefinger, he pulled, slow, drawing out the sound of the unraveling of caught teeth. The dress split, revealing the loose hills of her shoulders, aged freckles, and then, the pale tips of scars, and as he peeled her open, he discovered the crosshatches on her back, her map of pain, the healed tissue so thick it throbbed, and when it clicked, finished, he knew why she laughed when he told her he was just a desk clerk, why she said she didn't need a damn thing but kindness.

# WINGS

*by Guinotte Wise*

She lives in a stark house on flat prairie. No furniture. Her biplane is parked nearby. I don't think she has a self-preservation gene. I went up with her. At night. I don't fly, or I didn't until she got up on the top wing where she has this stanchion thing. That left me to guide the plane. She's a wing walker.

"It's not you," I said later. "It's me. I'm a wuss."

"Yeah, I kind of saw that," she said. Then she stripped and jumped into the big pile of brome hay. "Come on. It's tame, but it's a start."

# LISTENING

*by Charlie Stephens*

Through the peeling wall I can hear you snap your bones one by one. Tiny pings of destruction. In the morning you start with your feet: small bones are easier. By noon, when the rain comes down in sheets, and the last of the leaves die off, you have moved to your fibula, working up to your femur. Not yet 15, you have an ageless resilience towards suffering, calling upon ancient curses that burn themselves on the backs of my eyelids, a list of all the mistakes I have made. The ways I didn't protect you, and still am not.

# FAIR

*by Emily Haymans*

You promised to get me something if I beat you. Game after game, you rewarded yourself. Funnel cakes, spun sugar, ice cream slipping down paper cups.

I saw the mirrored house. It was like the movie you shouldn't have let me watch, when a girl's breath clouded on one of the mirrors, and the man with the knife snapped out from inside of it in a burst of silver triangles. I dropped your hand, my mouth watering.

Your voice echoed from glass, my name bouncing around corners like flashes of light. I did not stop for one second to answer.

# HOW SHE CAME AND WENT

*by Robert Gregory*

I have a wing on one side only, she told me one time.

Nakedness is not the same as clarity, she said. Here, I'll show you.

Now don't be a lazy boy, she'd say. Her long smile.

She was full of cream and whiskey some days, cold water and flakes of rust on others.

She often daydreamed stepping lightly through the forest like an animal, one that belonged there, just going about its business, not in a movie, no fancy soundtrack. So she said. I hope she went that way or something like. She did love to have her way.

# EPITHALAMION

*by Jonathan Penner*

See how, like bees, wedding guests swarm eager groom and tired bride, like pilgrim bees, their hive too populous, that ascend at sun-topped midday, drift and swivel like a windswept veil and fall on Mrs. Johnson's new flowerpot, waiting empty as a church after Sunday services, parishioners scattered, and Reverend Black headed hungrily home for lunch of thickly cut ham, sweet potatoes, peas that roll before his fork like severed heads amid terrible combat, which, see!—have already summoned congregations of vigilant ants, and with raucous caws the district's crows, gratified as wedding guests swarming tired bride and eager groom.

# NAMING

*by Jason Peck*

A book of names, five months before the birth, and I suggested Abigail for the baby. A full name, three soft syllables; a Hebrew word, meaning "my father rejoices." But no, he told me—he slept with an Abby once.

I ran my hands over my belly. I couldn't think of anything smart to say.

We tried out names all night. Christina, a Chrissy he met at a frat party. Katherine, a Katie picked up on New Year's Eve the month before we met. Kelly, Laurie, Terri.... By next morning, our child was still unnamed, and even a little forgotten.

# UNDER THE PIANO

*by Roberta Beary*

The piano's shawl hides me. Mom comes in, turns on the record player. Famous Opera Arias. Her favorite. The love seat's plastic squishes when she sits down. She's wearing her blue socks. The thick itchy ones. I stick my thumb in my mouth and close my eyes. Mom's record screeches out La donna è mobile. She thinks I scratched it but I didn't. Here it comes. La—-mobile. Mom sighs. It's the needle's fault. It made the scratch, not me. I want to tell her. But I don't. Liar, she'd say. I don't care. I'm invisible. Under the piano.

# I WAS FURNITURE

*by James McCready*

I can't recall much from my childhood. For all I know, I was a piece of furniture—an inanimate object. A cactus in its pot. A collection of pieces gathered through my mother's struggles—the burnt toaster left on the snow-covered roof, the shattered drinking glass, the missing sofa that left a void across from the television set, the colorless metal bunk beds, the full-sized mattress yearning for its own frame, boxes of nonessentials locked in the attic with the dead birds, the toy box overflowing with decapitated toys, and, of course, the hot iron left dangerously near the bed.

# LAST NIGHT, THE LITTLE DIPPER LOOKED LIKE THE WALGREENS PHARMACY CUP

*by Ethel Rohan*

On the street, I pass a man eating a sandwich and the waft of onion walks with me a while. The rattle of metal tags on a collar and I always have to look, make sure the dog isn't loose and fierce. Three weeks ago, my mother died and I thanked God. This week, a glance at her photograph reminds, feels like a slap to my heart. The cards, flowers, and phone calls have stopped. Already. I almost turn around on the street and return to the company of the smell of onion, offer my hand for it to take.

# VIRGIN BIRTH, I

*by Myra Sklarew*

When Yiorgos was born he had already been staring at death for weeks. During Sofia's final contractions a pink hand appeared and then withdrew, making way for a tiny skull and, to the horror of the women in the room, a shriveled blue face. A face that Yiorgos had explored during the final days inside the womb of his mother. And against this body that his arm and legs first tested themselves in the waters of his mother's womb. Here that his identical twin brother took leave of this world and hung suspended there opposite Yiorgos like a bizarre talisman.

# THE WHITE ALBUM

*by Lee Romer Kaplan*

9,000 miles from their Galilean childhood, Amir drove north bearing gifts: white hydrangea from his seaside garden, and his version of the girl she'd been. Rifling through Lili's old photo albums, they found his mother making shakshouka; pretty Narda dancing, celebrating harvest. The sole image of Amir and Lili together—14, awkward, beautiful, they sit on his parents' sofa, Lili looking at the photographer, oblivious, Amir gazing only at her. Now, on the precipice of middle age, Lili willed Amir to kiss her, and when he did, opened her blouse for him to kiss the scar the bullet left behind.

# BY THE SEA

*by Barbara Goldberg*

How beautiful it is by the sea, even though there is war in the air, even though there is always war in the air, which makes people live with a vengeance. Road fatalities exceed those lost in battle. Children run wild—soon enough they will sleep on stones in the desert. In the sky planes fly lower than you would think possible, low enough to wipe your plate clean. There is an airport less than a mile away from the promenade and the sea, the beautiful sea, duplicitous in nature, licking your lips, wrapping its salty arms around your throat.

# YOU COULDN'T WAIT TO LEAVE THIS TOWN

*by Jennifer Handley*

Concrete steps rise from pebbly cracked sidewalks, but go, absurdly, nowhere. Into the boards of a fence, or the sunless dirt beneath a low tree limb. An empty lot. A telephone pole. Eighty years ago, a raging summer fire leveled everything for miles, and when the town returned, it shifted—just a little—and left these oddities. Growing up, I barely noticed. They were part of the salty, wind-bent landscape, pointless. Who cared?

But time passes. Smoke clears. Now I see: they're reminders, ways back. Someone lived here. And here. And here. The steps don't go nowhere. They go home.

# NEVER NINE

*by Rachel Fogarty-Oleson*

I.

II.
Like before: I kept a list of paper cuts and cramps—the sullen of (you) th—the taste of tin, the smell of antibiotics hemorrhaging at midnight.

III.
Minnow, you are a tiny butter pear, you quicken like a bruise.

IV.
You are still here and you weigh five ounces. The skins assemble a nest. The doctor tells me over the curl and swoop of telephone wire.

V.
Your metronome. Gypsophila. Sopravvissuto.

VI.
Braxton Hicks plays Let's Pretend. He's dressed in blue and white between splayed legs.

VII.
Chances slim. Jagged as a pinecone. Trickled Spring.

VIII.

IX.

# ALBERTO

*by Doug Cornett*

Alberto has all but forgotten everything.

"Do you remember that time..." he is asked, but the answer is invariably "no."

Occasionally, there are flashes: an amusement park whirring below him and the sound of wood against steel; the breath of an older woman with hungry lips; an angry morning in Pittsburgh. But, like all the rest, they are gone before long.

One morning, a long woman with hair the color of butterscotch stands on his front porch, begging for forgiveness with dark, sad eyes.

"It was such a long time ago," she pleads.

Alberto agrees, because she seems honest enough.

# BRUNO

*by Josh McCuen*

Bruno Ward, who told dirty jokes at the end of the bar; who was once arrested for screaming the Bill of Rights into a policeman's ear; who had four linear scars across his chest from when a grizzly bear attacked him; the individual with pale blue eyes and a long beard; who knew sea shanties even though he had never left the great state of Wyoming; Bruno, who was known to talk to himself when the snow became too much, who could make a three-course meal out of the forest behind his shack, has passed away after a long illness.

# LIL

*by Stephen D. Gutierrez*

Our neighbor Lil looked like a TV Indian, all sunbaked and leathery. She wandered the streets brokenly, ill dressed, barely attuned. She still recognized me. Then her calves grew putrescent and slowed her down.

And I learned about gangrene.

"She drinks a lot," my mother said. "She's so nice, poor Lil."

She and silver-haired Jess lived in a tidy two-bedroom across the street. Apparently, he drank too. "A lot. They're both so nice."

"They are."

"They're both Okies, you know. They've been through a lot."

When Lil set her kind eyes on me, all my teenage troubles vanished.

"They'll amputate."

# HEAT

*by Jane McDermott*

In the crazy yoga class it is fifteen hundred degrees and everyone acts like nothing's going on. Everyone moves through yoga postures, glistening like they've been dipped in Vaseline because it's fifteen hundred degrees in the room, but no one lets on that it's out of the ordinary.

When the class is small, the teacher gives instruction and walks around helping students make adjustments. When she came to help me as I struggled with a posture she asked me if I had any injuries.

"Well," I said. "I had a really difficult childhood."

"Remember to breathe," she offered. "Keep breathing."

# A DAY IN THE LIFE OF STEVE

*by Ashley Chantler*

Morning followers! Porridge as per! Another day, another dollop. Lol.

Dreamt again about H. Wizard!

Off to work!

On train opposite some lovely breasts. Milkydoodles! Trying not to lol.

In meeting. Yet another powerpoint presentation. Give me a rifle! #getmeoutofhere

Hey! Why do other people's packed lunches always look better than your own?

Who invented UHT milk? Genius.

Confused by spreadsheet. What's the diff between median and mean? #whogivesatoss

Hometime! Another day, another dollop. Lol.

More milkydoodles!

Welcome home, followers!

Who invented kievs? Genius. #steverecommends

Before the internet, life must have been mad!

Bedtime! The wizard awaits! Night night followers.

# HOUNDSTOOTH

*by Digby Beaumont*

Bernard checks the advice on the website again:

*1. Get close, but not too close. If the person sits and you stand, avoid having your crotch near their face.*

*2. Try to catch the person's eye, but don't stare, as this might make them nervous or even scared.*

*3. Start a conversation; ask a question requiring more than a 'yes' or 'no' answer. Be prepared to repeat yourself.*

8.02. The bus arrives in ten minutes. He prays she will be on it. In front of the hall mirror he adjusts his new houndstooth newsboy cap. It hides his monks' crown.

# THE WEDDING NIGHT

*by Jayne Martin*

Her knee slammed into the night table as she struggled to sit up. Outside, fog horns bellowed like beasts in search of their mates, while her bare foot brushed against the empty bottle of Jose Cuervo that had transported her from her own.

Her gaze fell upon the discarded heap of white satin. A swell of panic encased her in its grip: the pounding of the church organ, the suffocating scent of a thousand gardenias, the eyes—so many eyes—bearing down upon her every step.

From behind, she felt him stir, his arm slowly encircle her—like a noose.

# PROFILE

*by Andrew O. Dugas*

She slid the iPad across the counter so fast he had to catch it.

"What's the matter?" An all-too-familiar Facebook profile glowed up.

"Who is she?"

Before he could speak, she repeated "WHO IS SHE?" That manic edge that, he knew, no meds could dull.

"Honey, please. Please."

Her eyes flared, teeth gnashed. Once upon a time, he'd loved her wildness. Her craziness.

"Why are you SMILING? ARE YOU LAUGHING!" She slid backwards down the wall. "Why? Why? Why?"

He took the iPad and slid down next to her.

"Honey, look." His fingers enlarged the image. "It's you. It's you."

# MISSED CONNECTIONS > ANTARCTICA

*by Michael Mira*

I saw you sitting atop an iceberg yesterday. You were fishing. I was kayaking when I saw you and thought about paddling by to say hi, but you seemed intensely preoccupied. Some friendly advice: You're in the wrong area if you're trying to catch fish. You'll find better luck at -84.507816, -121.345314. You're the only woman I've seen out here for years … actually, the only other human being. I know this is silly, because I just made you up, but if you ever see this post, I would really like to share some hot chocolate with you and chat.

# THE END OF THE END

*by Stephen Cicirelli*

She asked sarcastically because she was afraid of what he really thought of her. He replied sarcastically because he was afraid of what she really thought of him. Later on his sofa, when they were both undressed and the wine was drunk, he said, "Can we just be serious for a minute?" She wasn't sure then if he was being sarcastic, so she said, "I'm sensing some real sarcasm there, champ." She said this sarcastically, too, stressing "sarcasm" and "champ," and smiling now, just in case he was serious about being serious, which she had no good reason to believe.

# COLOR THEORY

*by Leonard Kress*

Tommy did the hair of all the wives. Bouffants, streaks, highlights, henna, they came back every week. For some it was the way he'd agitate their nape before the blade grazed their neck, blowing bits of gossip into one ear, hooking hair around the other. For others—how he understood the quasi-spiritual qualities of color, as if taping a manifesto over ONLY YOUR HAIRDRESSER KNOWS FOR SURE posters, turning his shop into a nineteenth century Salon des Refusés. The play of light and shadow meant everything. "When do you want to look your best?" he'd wink. "In bed, I'd bet."

# THAT'S NOT LOVE?

*by Jon Sindell*

It was movie night, and the old Jewish milkman was asking his wife if she loved him after all of those years. With singing, of course. My wife grabbed my hand and squeezed it hard. When the song ended she turned and looked at me like, hey, we're like that too, aren't we? I smiled weakly. No sex again that night, just toddler time. Then at two I was jolted awake. The shouting came from a neighbor's apartment, all ragged and tender. "God damn it, you fucking bitch—I love you!" Well, maybe that's it. Christ, who the hell knows.

# IN AND OUT OF PLACE

*by Corey Mesler*

Another new year, they tell me. Trees laden with drippings, Pollock oaks. I venture onto the carpeted lawn with only a number two pencil. My neighbor with great legs beckons from her porch—she has a place of heat but no light. She wants me to invest that place with significance. Nights I hear her mewing.

Someday, and it can't come too soon, I will pack up my cassettes and head to the unknown palaces of sin, where flows the river of need. I have the children's wishes to guide me; I only have to reinvent myself along their lies.

# THE SELF IN ONE PART

*by Tsering Wangmo Dhompa*

I can be funnier than you. Purists, nudists, gravel placates nerves. Pulchritude, a word scheming as buxom does for a sensible language. I take advantage in italics. There is beauty: black bough on snow; a straight line; shore line, life—hello?

The effort of breathing is to get to the point: fate. Alas, a plot begins with future as character. This morning a ship entered my eyes moving so very slowly I did not notice I was twisting my body. I know you are thinking, breast.

Lately, the world swivels at will and I find I shut my eyes tight.

# JIMMY CONSIDERS THE SCAR ON THE TIP OF HIS RING FINGER

*by Jason Marak*

I ordered this sandwich once with paper-thin carrots in it. I can't remember what else. I tried to recreate it. I failed. There's transcendence when flesh comes against blade. The graphic contrast: red, white. It's exhilarating, touching something you mustn't. The instant before consequences (the sting, the blood) is sublime. Everything else in the world, in your head, is vaporized. I think that's why she left—pursuit of that moment. It requires that we come up against what we shouldn't. I don't think she wanted to do those things. It was just a slip of the knife and the need.

# IMAGINARY NUMBER

*by Shara Concepción*

Before the necktie hung itself, a knot doing unto me what the body did; before the engine, fuel wound, light, I was the instrument and the song, un-living on the vocal cord of God, an imaginary number on a line I couldn't see. And then it appeared, before I had a word for eye, before I had a word for word, the wide-open face of a ticking clock: that swaying drop of amber light, its tapered head a glowing dancer, disembodied, slick and soft. A darkened room, a window. A world behind it, waiting, like a box of scattered light.

# DESCENT

*by Levi Andrew Noe*

I tried to teach you how to shoot a spit wad. How to find the right shooter, just the right diameter. A pen will do in a pinch; it's easily concealed and disguised. I tried to show you the ropes of delinquency. Cheating gumball machines, firecrackers in the mailbox, where to hide and how to use the porno mag we stole from Dad. I gave you your first black eye, baseball glove, drink, smoke, concussion, G.I. Joe, bike ride in a lightning storm, and friendship. I did the best a brother could.

But I never taught you how to fly.

# TRUTH IS

*by Cherie Hunter Day*

I take a crow as a wife. She is faithful to the task. There are many words in her language for want. She has no tact but at least she's truthful. Her eyes were blue when we met but they now match the black weave of night. She's in it for the occasional disaster that involves the interstate. It's about the long haul, the short shrift, the culmination in I, me, and mine. We shag at sunrise when the cool air is calm and magnificent. In time our progeny spread out across the county, but we don't keep in touch.

# SLEEPTALK

*by Adrienne Pilon*

Even in his sleep he talked, keeping her awake throughout the night. During all the dark hours, during all his dreams, his face echoed the phrases he formed: mouth widening, lips moving, brows rising and falling, eyes squinting and opening. The hands held more: stretching, spinning, circling, waving, tracing arcs and swirls and angles above his supine body, a constant dance of words rising and falling with his long fingers on the air. Letters formed words formed sentences formed paragraphs formed stories. He rocked the bed with his talk. Each night she staggered to the floor, seasick, seeking silence, stillness.

# ROLLING

*by Dzvinia Orlowsky*

Late August, a black cat rolling in mown grass flips to its back again, then rolls to its feet, half sun-drunk, half whiplash tail. I am loved. Not. Am. I've mastered these tricks: at parties after my husband's *break a leg*, rolling an ice cube on my tongue, my eyes rolling over crowded rooms, my body buckled forward rolling over rolling words. Rolling my eyes, having blood drawn, the vial filling slowly as flood water rising. Rolling through one marriage then breaking it off, holing up, each of us rolling away into our second marriages pretending, yes, to be dead.

# ONE OF THOSE THINGS

*by Jackie Davis Martin*

She remembered the nearby precipice, the brambles needling through the red plaid blanket—a thin bedspread really—all-purpose in their car. She remembered begging him: pull over here, please—her body pulsing with a desire almost like pain—no one will see us. She remembered the release among barren pines, the ocean roaring below, the day coming into clear focus afterward, a California coast. Thirty years later they'd survived, as had the plaid spread, tucked into whatever car, now serving as a cradle for a potluck casserole, a bench pad at an outdoor concert. It came in handy, she remembered.

# REGARDING THE MUSE OR MY HUSBAND

*by Maria Pinto*

We rode a barrel over Niagara Falls as practice for riding night over the skyline. We forgot we had names and mothers. We did it without a drop of drink. We wrote "FOR A GOOD TIME CALL KALI" in dove's blood ink on bathroom stall walls, to test what she'd do. We became armchair neurosurgeons and rewired our brains so they led one to the other. We prayed so well we heard all the gods answer, each singing their part of the harmony with such sweet perfection our goosebumps lasted days. But that was a different time. Before the contracts.

# WHAT I AM NOT SAYING

*by Emma Bogdonoff*

Once you knew a boy and you loved him though you never said. Through so many years, you never said. It made you irreplaceable; who else could say so much with so few words? Together, you named every plant and place and animal. Instead of speaking of love, you spoke of Venice in autumn, of the cat in Istanbul. It was a language whose words were memories. It was inimitable. And yet. Now there are no memories, no places, no animals. Now there are no words with which to not say, I love you, to not say, please come back.

# THE TOAST

*by Heather Bourbeau*

The clinking of glasses as she clears tables will be what she remembers most clearly. Bell-like, clear, almost happy. She will take home her dirty apron, shower the scent of service off of her skin, finish the crossword half-done on her morning commute, and pour a glass of port. Winter frost nearly thawed, she will hear crickets, smile, and quickly forget their chirping. She will sleep for three hours and twenty-seven minutes before the choking smoke wakens her and the firemen help her out. She will stand, mute, in charred nightdress, and recall the last toast to her old life.

# NAKED

*by Nancy Stohlman*

The scissors slide easily through the thick denim of my favorite blue jeans, from ankle to waist, ankle to waist, as one leg and then the other falls away. He slices up the middle of my thin cotton shirt like tissue paper, unwraps me, my pink Victoria's Secret bra a final ribbon snipped and spilling to the ground, leaving me naked. Exposed.

Are you having trouble breathing? he asks with kind brown eyes.

A little, on one side, I whisper.

We'll be there soon he says, gently placing an oxygen mask as the ambulance sirens rattle the warm evening air.

# NAME THAT TUNE

*by Kermit Moyer*

As we came up over the hill, they started shooting at us from the woods. We hit the dirt and you could hear the bullets making a sound like buzzing insects as they whizzed by overhead. To my right, Henry made a moaning sound as if he'd been hit, but, no, he was just singing to himself. "What's that song?" I asked him. But he didn't answer. He probably couldn't hear me. The next thing I knew, we were on our feet running across the field toward the woods again, and I never did find out what that song was.

# WAR NEVER ENDS

*by Gail Hosking*

Night after night I scoop up fish in the shower. I carry them to safety and they swim out of my grown-up hands. In the morning it's still 1967 with the wretched work of war's dragons and my father's black body bag, forsaken imprints of my mother's red lipstick, a famine in her kitchen with a vinyl pocketbook of failure come down through the years. Night after night I want to show her the saved fish. Instead, I watch men on the sidelines count the fish, string them up, brag about the size and weight, then throw their bones away.

# DARK

*by Sarah Freligh*

She asked me once what's it like not to dream and I said: Nothing. Imagine nothing, the vast black of it. Like climbing into a mineshaft, the way my dad did every day until the earth opened up and swallowed him and a dozen other men. You're not your father, she insists. But I am. I'm his hands and his little toe, the same sideways curl to it. I have his eyebrows and mouth, his stomach for jalapeños, a thirst for raw whiskey from a jar. Every night, I climb into a mineshaft and fall into sleep, feeling my way.

# WAITING

*by Kathy Steblen*

Fourteen days holed up here with peels of wallpaper, like streamers, looping in mock festivity above my head. Today is my birthday marking 14 years, the past two weeks spent hiding in this carcass of wooden ribs, like Jonah, swallowed whole by a whale. The temperature dips, icing demolished cornstalks in the field, their season complete. My body's a cash crop, harvested yearlong. Javier's taunts echo like a dirge: *Eres mio. Never leave. I will find you.* Others visit here; they shoot-up, fuck, or sleep. We've struck a deal: leave me be, upstairs. When he finds me, I will jump.

# HECTOR'S RECORD COLLECTION

*by Fred Osuna*

Hector Gonzalez, feared by the neighborhood youth, lived in his family's garage and hung black lights on the big door, forcing us to sneak in from the back. We'd rifle through his records: Zappa, Santana, Clapton. I stole one I knew he wouldn't miss. After he found out, my sister got in his face, defending me. Hector swung a roller skate, grazing her scalp. Soon after, Mr. Gonzalez began parking his car in the garage, and we never saw Hector again. Today, on Facebook, I read that Hector was comatose. I spun the Watergate Comedy Hour LP to his memory.

# YOUTH IN ORBIT

*by Aaron Teel*

We wanted to be the first children in space, but by the time we finished building our rocket, we were very old and our hearts weren't in it anymore. We launched ourselves anyway, and our children's children's children were there to see us off.

Our children's children's children wanted to come, but our children's children thought it might not be safe, and anyway, we thought, why should they get to be the first children in space? Build your own damned rocket.

We listened while our children and our children's children and our children's children's children counted backward in the yard.

# SALIENT SOUNDS

*by Connor Walsh*

Back when I was young enough to invent and trust in my own Boy Scout knot, I tied a tape-recorder to a turtle's shell and set it free. The first hard rain must've broken the flimsy thing, but I like to pretend it recorded the rain without breaking. This way, if the turtle ever returned, I could listen to the salient sounds teeter throughout the hum of low-fidelity. Maybe I'd hear my voice as a child telling him not to go too far. Or maybe I'd only hear him passing through the tall grass and, very slowly, going too far.

# DIGGERS

*by Amy Lafferty*

In summertime we look for things buried in the clay. Our parents call us, but we lose their voices by digging deeper. We find arrowheads and campfire rings. Deeper, and we find Pleistocene glaciers, and past that, terrible feathered monsters. Deeper, and the town is an ocean floor. We drown as we dig until the earth is molten. We dig and burn until it crumbles to dust. We dig as the universe sucks its breath in to a single everything, and as that also fades, we dig still, like a stone into God's own heel, to find what came before.

# SPARK

*by Molly Fuller*

It has always been like this inside the woods: trees subdivide the sky, flowers track the sun, moss and stone make configurations along streambeds drying in summer's heat. Today there is a fastening and then an unfastening as three girls who play there become something else. Two transform themselves from girls to killers back into girls. They toss knives in the dry river like skipping rocks, shed bloodied clothing like pulling wings off a fly, dance like butterflies in dappled sunlight. They cover one's body with sticks, with stones, with dried leaves that crackle like tinder in their small fists.

# ON THE LAST DAY

*by Colin Lubner*

On the last day, we will open our door, step into the still air of uncreation, and watch the sky unfurl. We will walk down to Henrietta's Diner like every day before, order the same bagels, the same coffee, open our laptops, and watch all our writings unwrite themselves. Our history spelled out in caramel steam, our destruction written in cinnamon swirls. Out the window, atop the hill we have made our home, our house will stand white, constant; its backing sky will turn to first paper, then code, the universe retracting into the potential light that started it all.

# GONE

*by Gerri Brightwell*

The show-off Goldbergs went first—the middle of the night and their whole house swallowed up with a crash fit to wake the dead. Friday evening the Duponts' garage vanished, taking Mr. Dupont's Porsche that he wouldn't let his wife drive, and leaving a hole that was nothing but darkness that had a stink all its own.

On Sunday when the Universalist Church at the corner was taken, we knew what it meant, because what sort of a religion is that? Us, we got down on our knees and prayed, and we're praying still, while all around the earth trembles.

# ABOUT THE EDITORS

Grant Faulkner is the executive director of National Novel Writing Month and the co-founder of *100 Word Story*. His stories have appeared in dozens of literary magazines, including the *Gettysburg Review*, the *Southwest Review*, and *Five Points*. His essays on creativity have been published in *The New York Times, Poets & Writers, Writer's Digest,* and *The Writer*. He recently published a collection of one hundred 100-word stories, *Fissures*, and his 100-word stories have been included in *Best Small Fictions 2016* and *New Micro: Exceptionally Short Stories*. He's also published a book of essays on creativity, *Pep Talks for Writers: 52 Insights and Prompts to Boost Your Creative Mojo*, with Chronicle Books.

Lynn Mundell is the co-founder of *100 Word Story*. She has worked as a professional writer and editor for 30 years. Her poetry, creative nonfiction, and short stories have appeared in literary journals including *The Sun, Superstition Review, Eclectica, Tin House* online, *Portland Review*, and *Five Points*, and have been published in the

U.S., the U.K., New Zealand, and Australia. She is most recently a contributor to the W.W. Norton anthology *New Micro: Exceptionally Short Stories.*

Beret Olsen is a writer, photographer, and the photo editor for *100 Word Story.* Her art, essays, and fiction have been published in a variety of places including: *First Class Lit, Flash: The International Short-Short Story Magazine*, and her blog, Bad Parenting 101. A longtime educator, Beret also writes grants to help low-income, first-generation college students get into, through, and beyond college.

To learn more about
the contributors to
*Nothing Short Of,*
visit 100WordStory.org
or outpost19.com/NothingShortOf.

CPSIA information can be obtained
at www.ICGtesting.com
Printed in the USA
BVHW03s0844140818
524457BV00025B/21/P

9 781944 853488